Voices of Minnesota History

VOICES OF MINNESOTA HISTORY

1836–1946

Bonnie Beatson Palmquist

2000
Galde Press, Inc.
Lakeville, Minnesota, U.S.A.

Voices of Minnesota History
© Copyright 2000 by Bonnie Beatson Palmquist. All rights reserved. Printed in Canada.
No part of this book may be used or reproduced in any manner whatsoever without written permission from the publishers except in the case of brief quotations embodied in critical articles and reviews.

First Edition • First Printing, 2000

Cover photograph of old Mendota Church, June 1904, by E. C. Oswald. Reproduced with permission of Minnesota Historical Society

These voices are based on material found in the Minnesota Historical Society's Manuscript, Archives, and Sound and Visual Collections. The Irwin Shepard Papers are now housed at the Bentley Library, Ann Arbor, Michigan. One poem is based on other sources. All photographs are from the Society's collections.

"They Troubled Me So Bad" appeared in the Spring 1994 issue of *Hennepin County History*

Library of Congress Cataloging-in-Publication Data
Voices of Minnesota history, 1834–1946 / [compiled by] Bonnie Beatson Palmquist.—1st ed.
   p. cm.
 ISBN 1–880090–89–0 (pbk.)
  1. Minnesota—History—Anecdotes.   2. Minnesota—History—Sources.   3. Minnesota—Biography.
 I. Palmquist, Bonnie Beatson, 1929–

F606.6 .V65 1999
977.6—dc21
                        99–045484

Galde Press, Inc.
PO Box 460
Lakeville, Minnesota 55044–0460

For Deborah Keenan

Contents

Introduction — xiii

I. George Franklin Turner, 1806–1854:
   The Wind Is East — 1

II. Found in the Charles A. Ames and Family Papers:
   Three Voices From the Slave Market — 11

III. Sarah Jane Christie Stevens, 1844–1919:
   My Dear Father — 23

IV. Irwin W. Shepard, 1843–1916:
   Flag of Truce: November 20, 1863 — 29

V. Emily Warren Todd Mitchell, 1824–:
   They Troubled Me So Bad — 39

VI. Elizabeth Carver Rankin/Lillian Carver Brown:
Indenture   49

VII. From the Death Records of Redwood County:
No Voices Call "Mama"   71

VIII. Photograph:
Orphan Train   83

IX. Thomas Davidson Christie, 1843–1921:
Precious Relics   89

X. Anne Grant Barry, 1825–1906:
The Woman Who Haunts Me: Great-Grandmother   99

XI. Carmelite Brewer Christie, 1852–1931:
A Pandemonium of Sound   107

XII. Recollections of Survivors of the Cloquet Fire:
    Flames Roared in the Wind; October 12, 1918   123

XIII. From the Papers of Ruth Mura Tanbara:
    American Born   133

XIV. The British War Relief Society:
    Dear Ladies of America   143

Introduction

A manuscript cataloger at the Minnesota Historical Society for twenty years, I have read many letters and diaries that I felt deserved a wider audience than the few researchers who might see the collection. I have used such original material as a basis for poetry (somewhat akin to a novelist writing a story based on historical events). The process of making primary sources more approachable may result in a poem or story taken entirely from those sources but presented in edited form; or the writer may add details or background rooted in research. This break with tradition is a recognition that history is told in many ways.

These pieces use material from the Minnesota Historical Society and the Bentley Library in Ann Arbor, Michigan. I have used primary sources either as a springboard for my work or in some cases put the writer's voice from diary entries or letters in a another form. I have indicated the origin of each segment, and whether I used the person's own words, my interpretation of them, or a combination of both.

One can read this book chronologically, from the Seminole War to World War II. We can trace the trail of children who were sold, abandoned, separated, orphaned, died or were never born. We might track the dramatic change in the lives of women from the 1860s to the present, women who had no voice, who knew knowledge was strength, who stood fast whether it was in Maple Grove, Minnesota, or Tarsus, Turkey. One can read of the plight of families who were separated and survived, while others were split forever by circumstances that

Voices of Minnesota History

foreshadowed events of today. Perhaps the greatest irony of World War II was that we sent clothes and goods to our allies in England, yet imprisoned our own Japanese-American citizens by the thousands, who in turn had to request their own goods to be sent to them in the relocation camps.

Voices from the past challenge us to remember they come from people who lived, loved, and left a record of their lives, even if it was only a few lines on a census page. These manuscript collections, letters, and diaries contain words that have remained with me. The thoughts are honest and powerful. I was drawn to them in my belief that their involvement in the world in which they lived was not so different from our own. Their experiences were small scenes of survival played against the screen of scholarly history. These light and dark threads—of courage, sorrow, and loneliness—weave a rich tapestry background for our own experiences.

I have tried to remain faithful to these voices heard faintly from long blue paper, scribbled pencil diary entries, and elegant flowing script now encased in gray boxes.

—Bonnie Beatson Palmquist

I. George Franklin Turner, 1806–1854: The Wind Is East

George Franklin Turner, 1806–1854

The last century with its many wars and military actions has separated families in many ways. It was a strain on relationships making them stronger or dissolving them. The separation of military families was the same in the 1830s as today. I found myself admiring George and Mary Turner for maintaining their relationship through the most trying situations.

George Turner wrote long letters to his wife, Mary (Molly) while they were separated. He was a keen observer of human nature; his letters from Florida showed sympathy toward the Seminole Indians and African slaves. Letters exchanged made the long distances seem even greater with the slowness of the mail. He missed his family and tried to close the distance with long letters containing descriptions of his life, quarters, wildlife, and fauna.

George Turner was born in Boston April 22, 1806. He graduated from Harvard University in 1826 and Harvard Medical School in 1830. Commissioned an assistant surgeon in the U.S. Army on July 23, 1833, he was sent to Fort Mackinac, Michigan. It was there he met Mary (Molly) Stuart, daughter of Robert Stuart of the American Fur Company. His assignments went from Michigan to Castle Pinckney, South Carolina, to Florida, where he was stationed from February 1836 to July 1839.

Mary was a spirited woman who followed him on assignment when she could. The conditions she faced would have daunted a more timid woman. She was not the only woman to do so, although some women preferred to remain in one place while their husbands were on active duty. She learned to be resourceful; at one point, unable to procure shoes in Texas, she sent for material and made her own.

The following composite letter uses direct quotes from his letters written during the time (1836–1839) they were separated, when he was in Florida and she in Detroit.

The Wind Is East

I.
I left you, my dear Molly, with an aching heart.
   God grant in his mercy that our separation
      may be blessed to us. Kiss my dear baby.

Does our darling behave her little self
   as well as when her father was with her?
      Does she talk as much? I suppose she will walk in
         a few weeks.

I had just begun to love her when I was obliged to leave.
   The wind is east as I said before
      and I feel a very distinct rising
         up as I have done before;

it is a symptom of Nostalgia vulgo homesickness.
   This life of single blessedness does not agree with me
      although I have tried hard to think it did.

Could I look forward each week to the receipt
   of a letter from you, I am sure the time would not
      hang so heavily on my hands. You know how unfortunate

your letters to me have hitherto been.
   I hope you may be able to devise some scheme by which
      they may be regularly written,

and when written regularly *put into* the Post Office
   for you know, dear Molly, that this part
      of the arrangement is quite necessary in order
         that I might get them.

The Wind Is East

I am guilty each day of the sin of wishing days,
   weeks, and months could be taken from time,
     that I might be brought nearer to the period
        when I trust we may meet once again.

My house looks clean, no nightgowns, no nightcaps or rags
   of any kind on the bed or floor, no pins or needles
     between the sheets, oh how delightful it is to live
        as a bachelor.

I am afraid to begin talking of home and comforts
   of domestic life, of our dear baby and her interesting
     tricks, for all such thoughts
        make me sad, make me think of *resigning* again.

I hardly know an officer who is not about to resign
or else thinking seriously about it. I am thinking
seriously on the subject *myself.* I cannot feel
resigned to absent myself from all I hold
most dear for years.

The life I am now leading together with the prospect
of being buried alive in a little fort surrounded
by Indians, to be subjected to all the ills
of danger, sickness, and separation
from my dear little family is more
than I can endure.

I hope to be with you soon, do strive to be composed
if you love me. May the Lord preserve our darling child.
I look to the arrival of the next mail with extreme
anxiety.

II.
I am today rather dull owing to several circumstances,
   the principle of which is the annoyance and fatigue
     of attending to about 130 sick who have arrived
        here from Ft. Drane and Micanpy.

The generals did not like to stop overnight
  at such a savage place as this, but needs return
    immediately after the ceremony of landing,
      and viewing the battleground was over.

The Dragoon Band accompanied this august party.
  The effect of a full band here in the wilderness
    was upon me most remarkable
      (you know my sensibilities)

I believe I had the *hysterics,* I could have cried
   had I not been ashamed, and could have laughed
     had I not feared that I might cry.

Fortunately no airs were played which called up
   any very peculiar associations. Do you know that
     "Come to the Sunset Tree " and "On the Margin
        of fair Zunard Waters" are sure to awaken a thousand

reminiscences of past joys. The latter is Billy's favorite
   and the former I used to sing with Miss M. E. Stuart
     some twenty years ago.

III.
Wolves again most hideous howling, yelping, screaming,
   barking just outside the pickets. I believe they usually
     perform their weekly serenade on the nights I devote

The Wind Is East

to writing to you. Well, we are both satisfied,
   they make music and I attend to my letter.

Our room is gloomy enough, and rendered particularly
   by the presence on every hand of those things
     which tend most forcibly to remind me

of you and Billy. The little shoes sit on the window as you
     left them. The cloak hangs on the door.

I look up at the window to see the baby and hear his funny
   little voice. I had no idea I could miss you so much.
     Good night Molly. I hope you will sleep as soundly
       as if I were with you to share your bed.
         Your devoted husband, George F. Turner.

Slave quarters, Helena, Arkansas; taken while the 6th Minnesota Volunteers were camped in Helena in 1864.

Photo by T. W. Bankes

reproduced with permission of Minnesota Historical Society

II. Found in the Charles A. Ames Papers: Three Voices From the Slave Market

Found in the Charles W. Ames and Family Papers: A Long Blue Envelope

Manuscript collections often have unexpected contents not related to the subjects expected. In a long blue envelope marked in faint pencil, "For Charles W. Ames from Maria Cary," were several letters, ledgers sheets, and promissory notes. From these few items, a glimpse of life in two slave markets appear. Slaves were separated from family members, children from their mothers, wives from husbands. Considered an item of wealth, the casual decisions to sell and buy are hinted at in the contents of the envelope.

It was an eerie feeling holding these few items documenting the buying and selling of human beings. Were this woman and her child separated? How callous to underline the possibility of taking her two-year-old child from her! I found myself wondering whose story was told in these few scraps of paper.

How this envelope came to be in the Charles Ames Papers is unknown, but the family was known to be sympathetic to the abolitionist cause. Perhaps the material was given to them as evidence of the slave trade. This material was the basis of "Three Voices From the Slave Market."

Three Voices From the Slave Market

I. The Inquiry: L. P. Olos

Hillsboro, NC
Oct 3 1861

"What could I get for a strong healthy woman a pretty good cook washer & ironer, about 35 years old, with or *without* a girl child two years old."

L. P. Olos

Clarissa Speaks:

Child, don't look at me like that,
your eyes as dark as my thoughts.

Too young to know this is how it is,
never knowing when master will sell.

Never knowing when your family's gone,
mother, sisters, husband.

They took your sisters so long ago.
Their faces fade like first early light.

Can't love them too much, for my heart is
as heavy as the unseen chains around us.

Three Voices From the Slave Market

I hold you as the night clings to darkness
to shield itself from the terrors.

Child, what will happen to you
when the dawn comes and claims its own?

Sleep now, my arms hold all of you,
the lost ones with small shadows,

whose silent voices demand I remember
until all are gathered in your small face.

II. The Buyer: Henry Easley

Richmond March 14\63

"Due E. H. Stokes three thousand dollars borrowed to invest in negroes for his sale."

Henry Easley

Three Voices From the Slave Market

Henry Speaks:

The fields need planting, fences mending.
I ride the boundaries,
see the neglect of Ashby Place.
My father built this plantation,

hired master craftsmen,
bought the finest furniture,
thoroughbred horses from Ireland.
Ashby Place was known for its hospitality,

its lavish parties, a place for discussion
of local politics. A house of importance.
My whole life is here, and by God,
I will do anything to keep it.

I will keep my heritage,
my children's legacy.

This land is my identity.
It will not be taken by the damn Yankees.

I need young, strong backs
who see the sun rise,
feel the coolness of dusk,
all in a day's work.

10 or 12 year olds will do.
They won't be so eager to run.
Still I need house slaves,
ghosts roam Ashby Place,

recalling its glory days.
I fear the coming years.
But I will survive.
I can do nothing else
but live.

III.
The Slave Trader: E. H. Stokes, Richmond, Va.

E. H. Stokes Speaks:

Father began trading in the early '40s.
Shiploads came in shades of color,
shapes; wailing or mute.

Though I've seen eyes flash
hatred from the proud ones,
those who knew their fate.

I met a slave ship once.
Its stench heralded its arrival.
I wouldn't meet another one.

A business I'm expected to follow,
like selling cotton,
only my merchandise picks it.

But I board them, dress them;
a hoop skirt for Lucy Ann,
a full suit clothes for Andrew.

To tell the truth, I'm weary of this,
selling human misery. For that's what it is.
Poor dumb beings, sold by their own people.

Mothers wail, plead, or stare stony face.
When it comes to sell the children.
"Can't love them too much"

Girls, twelve or thirteen, bring $700 to $800.
Seems owners want them young.
Offspring belong to the masters.

Three Voices From the Slave Market

Henry Easley invested three thousand dollars.
His plantation needs field hands,
all the strong backs are gone.

This week's sale went well,
I entered twelve sold in the ledger:
four girls, four boys, three men, and a woman,

Clarissa and her child.

Sarah Christie, 1861.

Original in
James Christie Collection

reproduced with permission of
Minnesota Historical Society

III. Sarah Jane Christie Stevens, 1844-1919: My Dear Father

Sarah Jane Christie Stevens, 1844–1919

Sarah Christie, born in Sion Mills, Ireland, to James and Eliza (Reid) Christie, came with her family when they emigrated to the United States and settled in Wisconsin. After country schools, she entered Fox Lake Seminary, where her education was paid in part by her brothers, William and Thomas, while they were serving in the Civil War. She graduated in 1863 and began teaching in nearby schools.

By 1873, she was teaching German and English literature at Carleton College in Northfield, Minnesota. From 1875 to 1877 she taught at Wheaton College, Wheaton, Illinois. She was 35 when in 1879 she married William Long Stevens, a widower with four children. They remained on his farm near Rapidan, Minnesota, where she gave birth to their two daughters.

After her marriage, she remained interested in education, particularly for her stepchildren. She became the first woman superintendent of schools in Blue Earth County, Minnesota, in 1890 and went so far as to order books in German for the children of the emigrants. She lost in the next election. Sarah died in 1919 in Minneapolis at the home of her daughter, Dr. Elizabeth Monahan.

The following are excerpts from a letter (November 11, 1862) to her father, James, when she makes an impassioned plea to be allowed to continue her schooling.

Sarah

My Dear Father, I am determined on having an education,
   and if I keep my health, I will have one
     if it takes me ten years or more
        to earn money for it.

I think therefore that it is my duty
   as well as the duty of others to improve
     as much as possible and to cultivate my
       mind to be a Teacher to others.

It is my highest ambition in this world,
   and if I keep strength and health,
     I am to have an education if I am
       thirty years of age before
         it is finished.

You speak of Algebra as being
  a "masculine attainment."
    I cannot see as it is any more
      than a "Feminine attainment."

Now I cannot see how it is that men
  will think that they are any better
    fitted for the duties of life
      than women and that their powers are stronger.

They think that they are a little bit more elevated
  and look at everything from a higher place,
    and are, in fact, a few inches taller.
      But it is they who keep women where they are.

It is the education which a woman gets and the false Ideas
  that are crammed into them, that keep women
    where they are. Now I believe that the weakness
      of women lies in their education.

Sarah

They have the same powers given
   them that is [sic] given to man and if they were cultivated
     and strengthened, in the same way and Direction,
       woman would be just as able to make her way
         through life as man is.

To be sure there would be a great many
   who could not. But let each have a fair trial
     and those who are not able for it,
       let them fall back to their old place.

It really made me *vexed* when you said that
   Algebra was a *"Masculine" attainment* like as if
     I could not learn it as well as any *"Masculine"*
       I ever *saw* and maybe a great deal better
         than some, without killing me either.

If the women were rightly educated, as they should be,
> we would not read so much about that hackneyed phrase,
>> *"Women's Mission,"* nor hear it *"cursed"*
>>> so much about either.

I guess that if the *'Masculines"* got the same teaching
> and the same Ideas crammed into them which "Feminines"
>> get about not being anybody, they would be just
>>> as helpless, weak, vain, miserable things
>>>> as the generality of Females are.

I have not time to write you more as I have to write
> to Sandy and Van. So I hope that this will find
>> you all as usual. Give my love to Mother
>>> and the boys and to all Friends and believe me
>>>> your loving Daughter, Sarah J. Christie

IV. Irwin W. Shepard, 1843-1916: Flag of Truce: November 20, 1863

Irwin W. Shepard, 1843–1916

Irvin W. Shepard arrived in Minnesota in 1875 to serve as principal of Winona High School and, four years later, assumed the presidency of Winona State Teachers College. Beneath the archival information of this illustrious academic career lies the story of a soldier of the finest mettle.

In April 1862, Irwin enlisted with his cousin George in Company E, 17th Regiment, Michigan Infantry. In his letters (1862–1864) to his family in Chelsea, Michigan, he writes graphically of his experiences from the time of his enlistment to his participation in battles near Harpers Ferry, Fredericksburg, and Knoxville.

Awarded the Congressional Medal of Honor for his bravery during the November 20 action of the Battle of Knoxville, his citation read:

> Having voluntarily accompanied a small party to destroy buildings within the enemy's lines, whence sharpshooters had been firing, disregarded an order to retire, remained and completed the firing of the buildings, thus ensuring their total destruction; this at the imminent risk of his life from the fire of the advancing enemy.

His letter describing the event was written with his characteristic economy of words:

> On the night of Nov. 20 our Regt was detailed to drive a lot of Rebs from a large brick house they had got possession of and from which they were particularly troublesome and burn it and all the outbuildings. It was a very hazardous piece of business for we did not know how strong they were. We drove them in a charge without any trouble and set fire to the house and six other buildings (barns and sheds) after they got well to burning, we fell back having only two men killed and none wounded.

It is of the Battle of Knoxville and of the days following that action that he wrote the following selection.

A Flag of Truce: November 29, 1863

Two inches of mud, cold wind blowing
camp fire sputtering
orders to retreat, long way back.
Five times we sprang into battle,
alarms, but no battle.
Marched to the rear,
leaving a train of 80 wagons
of officers' baggage
for want of mules.
We got bacon, bread and sugar,
all we could carry
from the doomed train,
the last party set fire to it.
For miles we passed
heaps of commissary stores
giving up their comforts.

Then their troops
volleys whizzing over us.
On they came
their skirmish line
surrounded us,
fired on by three sides.
Every man ran for himself,
I threw off my knapsack,
I could no longer run.
My rubber, gun, and haversack,
was all I saved.

Supported by our 2nd division
we regrouped until artillery
from both sides
cut the trees to shreds.
Infantry draw back
from the barking mouths.

A Flag of Truce

Then in the open field
two lines of battle
came out, advancing,
nothing to oppose them.

All eyes on them,
the order to fire,
every shell burst in the right place
until lines broke
and ran like frightened sheep.

After ambulances passed
we walked.
I know every smooth piece of road
I went to sleep walking,
and did not wake up
until I stumbled or stepped
into a mud hole.

Hardly a word was spoken
the entire march.

About noon, the enemy came up,
and began to skirmish,
cut our communication.
We dig rifle pits all day
formed an impregnable line.
Rebel sharpshooters
entrenched themselves.
We were obliged
to live in the pits.

Our ration cut to 1/2 of meat,
1/4 of bread and what bread it is!
A mixture of graham flour,
corn and cob meal and molasses,
it was black and solid,

A Flag of Truce

a fist size piece
a day's ration.

November 29, Sunday morning,
a desperate charge,
with terrible slaughter.

A flag of truce until 7 at night.
We carried their dead to them,
their wounded to our own hospital.

We met on neutral ground
with the utmost friendliness.
We talked of South Mountain,
Fredericksburg, and Antietam
where we had fought each other.
We told them we were sorry
to have to slaughter them

as we had this morning.
They in return assured us
it was painful to shoot us.
How sincere their feelings were,
I will not try to tell.

Every day after this truce
the skirmishers on both sides
would if by common consent
cease firing at dusk,
come out of the pits,
get firewood
stir around and such,
relying on each other's
sense of honor *not to shoot*.
In no case that I know of
was this trust violated.

A Flag of Truce

At such times there was
a great deal of talking,
laughing, joking,
carried on between them.
Occasional visits made
to each other's pits
(although this was against
General Orders)
They would caution each other
to lie low as they didn't want
to hurt anybody when they
resumed the pits in the morning.
Five minutes after if either side
exposed his person,
a dozen balls were sure
to tell him of it.

December 4, the welcome news,
the reinforcements arrived.
That night the Rebels left
bag and baggage.

We hope to see better times,
I am thankful for what
God has done for me
in preserving my life
through so much of danger

Best Love and do write often,
Affectionately yours,
Irwin.

V. Emily Warren Todd Mitchell, 1824–: They Troubled Me So Bad

Emily (Emma) Warren Todd Mitchell, 1824–

Emma Warren Todd was born in Kittery, Maine, in 1828. She married John Mitchell on December 11, 1848. They moved to Minnesota in 1855 with their children, Charles Henry (1851?) and Frederick Warren (1854), settling on a farm in Maple Grove Township, Hennepin County. At the time John enlisted on August 22, 1864, two more children had been born, Ida (1857) and George (1862).

When John Mitchell joined the Headquarters Company, 11th Regiment, Minnesota Volunteers (he received a bonus for doing so), he left the operation of the farm to Emily. Her only help came from the older two boys, Charles, thirteen, and Frederick, ten. The plight of women left to operate the farm, handle the finances, and raise the children is told in this woman's letters. John's advice to Emma about how to get the house ready for winter (mud put on the inside of the walls to keep it warmer) and about threshing and butchering helped, but she still had to rely on the neighbors' help. That winter was so long and cold, she had to stack firewood by her bed. For four weeks, she was unable to get to the road. To add to that, her teeth ached.

Her journey to Minneapolis from Maple Grove over rough and rutted roads in the cold month of March took fortitude and courage, aptitudes she would not have attributed to herself. The children learned early responsibility in doing the farm chores. When John returned in June 1865, they resumed their life on the farm. Census records show the farm being worked by their son Frederick and his wife, Ida. Nothing further is known about the family.

The following is taken from three of her letters found in the John Mitchell papers.

They Troubled Me So Bad

Maple Grove
March 1865

My Dear Beloved Husband

You will forgive me this time
for not writing to you
in the middle of this week as usual
when I tel you the reason.
As you requested and urged,
I did comply with your wishes.
I have had the teeth Ache few days past
and my face is badly swolen.
thursday knight I did not sleep
but very little they troubled me so bad.

A. P. Bell dentist office, Alexandria, Minnesota, 1876.

Photo by N. J. Trenham

reproduced with permission of Minnesota Historical Society

They Troubled Me So Bad

I believe I have more tooth ache
in the last six months than six years before.

In my last letters from you,
you urged me to go
and have something done with my teeth
if I could muster the courage
but my Dear how can I go alone among strangers,
and there was no one who could go with me

Knowing it to be the very best thing
I could do I made up my mind to go
and try it anyway.
When Mrs Briggs came over
I told her I wanted to go to town
before sugaring commenced,
well said she
"Mr. Briggs is agoing tomorrow

Office of Dr. A. E. Benjamin,
1527 East Franklin,
Minneapolis, 1898.

*reproduced with permission of
Minnesota Historical Society*

They Troubled Me So Bad

and you can go with him just as well as not"
and Mrs. Norton said
she would stay with the children.
So I got ready and went.
The travelling is very bad.
We started from Briggs about six
and got home last knight about seven.

When I first got into town [Minneapolis]
I went down to Mrs Arnells,
you recollect I told you
that she made me A visit
not long ago with Mrs Cannon
and she has false teeth so I thought
I would talk with her about them.
She was very kind,
offered to go with me
to the best dentist in town.

I inquired of several
they all seemed to recommend the same man.
His name is Bosman.
Mrs. Arnell introduced me to him.

I told him I wanted some drawn
and I did not know but all
if I could have courage
so I sat down
and he drew the upper ones
in about ten minutes.
I can not tel you how bad he hurt
for you know all about it.
But I stood it very well.
Mrs Arnell was afraid
I would faint but I did not.
She could not stand by me
but went into the other room

They Troubled Me So Bad

when the upper ones were out.
He told me I would have to wait
just as much longer to have false ones
in as I was having them out
for it would take six months anyway.

So I told him he might draw them
and I dont think it was five minutes
when every one was out
21 roots and all.

They thought I had A great deal of courage.
He charged me five dollars for drawing them.

I may say it took away my appetite
for I have not ate any thing to speak of since.
I suppose it is well enough
for I dont see how I could eat

until they get better.
I took some cold coming home.
I was just as carefull as could be
but you know it was A long road
to ride in the cold
and they bled badly
and I had to undo my mouth
to spit all the way home.

I feel weary today,
they bleed badly
which makes me feel sick.

I shall write you again next Sunday.
Receive this from your ever faithfull

Emily Mitchell.

VI. Elizabeth Carver Rankin/Lillian Carver Brown: Indenture

Elizabeth Carver Rankin/Lillian Carver Brown

"Indenture" is based on the diary entries of Elizabeth Carver Rankin and a reminiscence of her daughter, Lillian Carver Brown, found in the Lillian Brown and Family Papers.

Charities were few in the 1870s. Families faced stress then as now, and there was no place to turn when they were in trouble. If family members or close friends were not there or were not supportive during times of trial, what happened to families that came apart? This is what happened to one family when the father left and four small children were more than their mother could manage.

A small legal notice, undated and not identified, caught my eye when I began this collection. Later, it disappeared, but the words were indelibly etched in my mind. Original words from letters, diary entries, and Lillian's reminiscences are shown in italics. The rest of the words are mine.

Indenture

Note of indenture: Elizabeth Carver indentures
Albert Carver, age one year,
for the period of ten years.

Austin Minnesota 1873.

RECORDER:
How were you
to raise them
after Edward left?
You never had
to keep house, sew, clean,
had no one
to help you.
Four children

taken by strangers.
How your heart
must have ached
to see them go.

Albert, still at the breast,
Lillie not yet three,
Willie seven, Eddie five.

You were seventeen
when you met him.
Every Sunday morning
your organ playing
accompanied his deep voice.
Then the war,
you waited
until he returned
from Andersonville.

Indenture

In love and carefree,
eager to be together,
you ran away.
Father's telegram,
"Wait until I get home,"
found you married,
he without a job,
you without a home,
just the two of you.

ELIZABETH:
Little did I then think
of the trouble
that was in store for me.

RECORDER:
Brought up by wealthy parents,
who had sheltered you.
Your Mother now dead
who would have helped you.
Your father remarried
and helpful no longer.

Babies coming,
floors to mop,
clothes to clean,
and you wanted
to visit neighbors,
play the organ;
be young again.

Indenture

ELIZABETH:
My mind goes back
to the day Albert was born
and I feel sad
as I remember the cruel treatment
I received from his father.

RECORDER:
He left,
said he'd send money, told you:
keep the children together.
But you didn't.

You must have known
what lay ahead
for them.

ELIZABETH:
How I regretted that decision,
made hastily,
and with bitterness toward him.

RECORDER:
Years passed.
You married again,
badly.
Your punishment?

ELIZABETH:
I am almost barefoot, my clothes are rags,
and he don't care as long as his gut
is stuffed three times a day.
A white woman is a fool
to marry a Johnny Bull.
There is no refinement

Indenture

or feeling about them.
All they care for is their own comfort.
I've lived with two of them
and they are both alike in that respect.
A woman throws her love away
when she marries one.

The years seem long.
I write long letters to the children
and wait for their letters
that come slowly,
reluctantly.

There is a longing at times,
to see their dear faces,
and it seems as if I could
not stand it to be separated
from them longer

but I know God will do all things well
and upon him I place my trust.
I feel He will answer my prayers
in His own good time.

Forgive me, children.

RECORDER:
And they did. Willie, most of all,
cared for his mother until she died.
Eddie gave her diaries
to ease her loneliness.
Bertie signed the pledge,
knowing the happiness it gave her.
Lillian, a daughter's forgiveness.

Indenture

ELIZABETH:
It is well ordained
that we do not
know the future.

Edward Carver

EDWARD:
Neighbor and friend,
I come to you,
I cannot stand
it any longer.
This gun will end
my despair.

If I stay,
here will be more babies.

RECORDER:
You were engaged
before you left
for the war.
Captured, then
the horror of Andersonville,
the thirst,
hunger, and sickness
felled your fellow prisoners.
No water, boiling sun,
you prayed, and then
in the corner, a splash
of water to save you.

Elizabeth waited for you.
She, with the dancing eyes,
the tiny waist,
the loving arms.

Indenture

You ran away,
were married
April 26, 1866,
by Reverend Raymond
in Chicago.

Her father gave you a job
with the railway.
You were a good worker,
advanced to be
a car inspector
in Minneapolis.
Then came the babies,
the crowded apartment.

EDWARD:
I could not stand the mess.
I could not bring my friends home

to join in the singing.
I prided myself
on my neat appearance,
impossible in that house.

RECORDER:
It was said
that you loved someone else,
but you never said
if that was true,
only that you had to leave.

EDWARD:
Friend, listen and understand.
You say,
"A terrible thing to leave
four little children."
And then you took the gun
and my release.

*I will send back money
for her and the children.
I would rather wade
in blood to my knees
than have my children separated.*

Lillie Carver

LILLIE:

*On December 10, 1873,
John and Ellen Mills
took me to their farm
outside of Austin.
I was two years, nine months.*

RECORDER:

*You were to replace
their daughter who died.*

LILLIE:
My childhood was very dull.
I had to work hard, very young.
I was expected to wash the dishes,
even though I needed a box to stand on.

When I was eight,
I started to school,
walking through heavy timber,
afraid of the wolves
who claimed that ground.

There was no sign of affection
in that family.
I was not allowed to have friends.
My only companion
was Jack, a shepherd dog.

Indenture

*My memories are sketchy.
I remember on moonlight nights,
staring into the dark shell
of the sky
hoping, waiting for God
to speak to me.*

*I was sixteen
when I left that house,
with only my family Bible.*

RECORDER:
You never replaced the daughter.
Years later, a letter arrived.

EDWARD:
*"You will probably be surprised
at receiving this from me.*

*I would have liked
to have seen you and Willie
when you passed through here.
But did not know
that you cared to see me.*

*"Now for what you
think my duty is,
my child if there is anything
under the sun that I can do
for you or the others
tell me what it is
and if in my power
will do it with pleasure.*

*"If you would like to hear
from me after thinking
about this write me*

and I shall be very much pleased
to hear from you
or the others at any time.
With love to you all,
I am your affectionate father, E. E. Carver."

LILLIE:
Yes, I want to see you,
after all, you are my father.
A neighbor told me you were a good man.
You had a lot to put up with.

RECORDER:
This neighbor said Elizabeth
did not know how to keep house,
swept the dirt into the corner.
Left the children to visit neighbors.
Willie and Eddie ruined the organ

by pouring water in it.
"Poor Lillie, cold and crying
on the porch when I saw you,
I reached through the window
and pulled your Mother's wedding dress
of blue taffeta and put it around you."

LILLIE:
Poor Mother, raised in a home of luxury,
popular in young society
in New York City,
then married to a poor man,
four little children
and absolutely no foundation
for facing life and then left alone.

Indenture

RECORDER:
Both of the parents
with their own demons,
lived with rash decisions,
denied their children a family.
Who speaks for their children?
Given away like unwanted toys.

Elizabeth left Austin, then returned.
In 1879 she married Mr. Rankin,
who had a farm at Saint's Rest
outside of Austin.

Edward went to Grand Rapids, Michigan,
worked on the railroad,
married Alice Churchill in 1883.

The children scattered,
all in different families
until they could leave.

Willie and Lillie found each other,
Bertie was farther away,
Eddie joined them later.
Never to live together,
but not as orphans either.
And they did forgive.

The children survived.
They inherited an inner strength,
tested in Andersonville;
a childlike hope for the future;
and faith stronger than their parents.

VII. From the Death Records of Redwood County: No Voices Call "Mama"

From the Death Records of Redwood County

A rchives are thought to be dry and dusty, but volumes stored and forgotten hold reality. In the nineteenth century, disease came in waves, rolled over settlements, and went on to the next victims. So it was in Redwood Falls County in the summer of 1884. Three families were affected, all devastated by the scourge of scarlet fever.

This was not an isolated occurrence. Children's deaths from many causes were expected in a family. One father cautioned his son not to love a child until it had reached the age of two, so when you lost it, the loss would not hurt so much. The son replied, "How could you not love the child, even if it meant the heartbreak of losing your first-born child?"

Death Register, village of Redwood Falls, 1884–1885.

reproduced with permission of Minnesota Historical Society

From the Death Records of Redwood County

I could not imagine the misery of losing all of your children, watching for the first fatal signs of the disease. How did the Lyss parents survive from day to day? How did the children endure watching their brothers and sisters die and knowing they might be next?

The following is based on the Redwood County record of 1884. Further research showed that the Lyss family had another daughter in 1886.

No Voices Call "Mama"

I.
The Children of the Lyss family,
   small and terribly poor,
      fell victim to the scourge

of the "strawberry" tongue,
   sore throat, flushed face.
      All signs of scarlet fever.

Henry J. Lyss, age 8, died Thursday
   June 12. Henry was a merry boy,
      black haired, blue eyes.

Pauline M. Lyss, age 1, died Sunday
   June 15. She had curly hair,
      a sweet smile, and dimples.

George M. Lyss, age 6, died Tuesday,
   June 17. A quiet boy,
     who followed his brother, Henry.

Frank W. Lyss, age 4, died Wednesday
   June 18. A friendly boy,
     who liked to play outdoors.

Annie C. B. Lyss, age 11, died Monday
   June 23. Pretty, dark-haired,
     shy smile, her mother's helper.

Mary Lyss, age 9, died Friday
   July 4. A younger version
     of her sister, Annie.

No Voices Call "Mama"

II.
Henry Lyss in his small shop doorway
   listens for the young voices
      heard only in memory.

The soundless wind nudges the rope swing.
   Ghostly laughter drifts to the ground
      as silence steals the evening.

In three weeks the scourge had
   decimated the dreams and hopes
      he brought from Bern.

He straightens his shoulders.
   His blue eyes look inward.
      Suddenly there is only he and Anna,
         again.

III.
Anna Lyss in her kitchen,
   cooks for two, unable
      to reduce the proportions.

Her big pot mocks her,
   soup covers only the black bottom,
      leaving a space that can't be filled.

Her handmade quilts lay
   smooth on the children's beds,
      no bumps, no wrinkles.

She finds a small rag doll
   with a weeping eye,
      guarding the last few possessions.

No Voices Call "Mama"

No cry in the night,
   no voices call "Mama,"
      only the creak of the wind

blowing through the cracks
   leaving a cold
      no warmth can melt.

She is stronger then she knows.
   Not like the other mother
      who walks into the lake in despair
         when the last of her children
            are gone.

IV.
Charles Schmit, Clerk of Court,
   on this clear, cold last day of December,
     sits in a brown leather chair,

in a room of dark wood and shelves
   holding leather-bound books,
     recording events of the town

of Redwood Falls. Everyday
   facts recorded in a firm hand.
     Hidden stories in black and white

on pages, pristine
   as the snow mounded against
     its red brick courthouse.

No Voices Call "Mama"

Births, deaths, and land sales
   to form the fabric
      of a small rural town.

He picks up a pen and begins to
   register the year's sadness.

Young girl, c. 1886.

Photo by Carlson and Wold

reproduced with permission of Minnesota Historical Society

VIII. Photograph: Orphan Train

Orphan Trains

From 1854 to the 1920s, thousands of orphaned, destitute, and unwanted children made the journey from East Coast slums to the Midwest on trains that became known as the Orphan or Baby Trains. The idea for them came from a minister, Charles Loring Brace, who saw the plight of thousands of street kids left to fend for themselves. He founded the Children's Aid Society in 1853 to care for these children. Not all children were orphans; some had been taken away from abusive parents, while others had been given up by poor families unable to care for one more child.

Accompanied by chaperones, the trains made their way into small towns all across the Midwest, where they were met by townsfolk and farmers ready to choose a child for their families. Lined up in their best clothes while the chaperone gave their names and ages, the children waited until their names were called out.

Most of the adoptions gave the children a better life than they would have had in the cities. A governor, two congressmen, twenty-three bankers, and a state supreme court justice were former wards of the Children's Home Society. There were, however, some abuses of the system.

These children, even as they found homes in the Midwest, would later wonder about their biological parents, if they had siblings, and why they were given up. Many would find no answers. They would create a life for themselves, which started on a train trailing steam and coal smoke into the prairie sky and disappeared into the unknown tomorrow.

Orphan Train

April 1893

Look at me, please!
You know why I am here
or you wouldn't have come.

They found us alone
after mama died. I tried,
really I tried, to keep
them fed and clean,
but then there wasn't any food
and they took us away.

Finally, a hundred of us
boarded the train
and began our journey west.

It's been long.
I tried to take care
of Willie and Mary
(she's three and is forgetting
Mama already).
I combed her hair
into ringlets so someone would
think she's pretty
and take her.
I didn't know that her cry
would cut through my heart
when, in Weston,
someone did.

I held Willie's hand as
we got on the train,
his tears streaming
down his cheeks.

Orphan Train

"Don't cry," I said.
We knew we probably
wouldn't be together.
But I had so hoped we would.
Then another stop,
this time in Milltown,
and we got off,
lined up in a row,
and a woman rushed
toward Willie
crying, "That's my Henry!"
"But that's not his name,"
I cried softly.
With a backward look
with those sad eyes,
he followed them.

That left me.

The matron pulled my hair back,
she said that it had a
"no nonsense" look
and someone would think
I was a good worker.
But we are nearing the end
of our journey,
so please look at me.
I need a home, I'll work,
but don't let me be
the last one.

IX. Thomas Davidson Christie, 1843–1921: Precious Relics

Thomas Davidson Christie, 1843–1921

Thomas Davidson Christie was a member of a remarkable family of James and Eliza (Reid) Christie, who immigrated from Ireland in 1846, settling in Wisconsin and later Minnesota. An insatiable reader, Thomas once commented that his family had the finest library of any farm home in Wisconsin. A writer of great perception and wit, his interests ranged from archaeology to his family's roots in Ireland and Scotland.

In October 1861 he and his brother William enlisted at Fort Snelling in the First Minnesota Battery of Light Artillery, in which they served until 1865. These were the brothers whose Civil War service helped finance the education of their sister, Sarah (p. 23).

After graduating from Beloit College in 1871, Thomas enrolled in Andover Seminary in Massachusetts and was ordained a Congregational minister. He saw the ministry as his calling in life and pursued it earnestly.

Thomas Davidson Christie, D.D., L.L.D., President of St. Paul's Institute, Tarsus, Turkey.

Photo by Randall Abbott of New Haven, Connecticut

From the Thomas and Carmelite Christie and Family Papers

reproduced with permission of Minnesota Historical Society

Thomas Davidson Christie, 1843–1921

In September 1877, he and his wife, Carmelite, along with family, left for Marash, Turkey, where they spent sixteen years in missionary work. In 1893, they moved to Tarsus, Turkey, where Thomas assumed the presidency of St. Paul's Institute. The Institute was under the patronage of Col. Elliot Shepard of New York City, who died soon afterward and left the college without adequate funding, which obligated the Christies to continually seek funds for the school. It was on one of these fund-raising trips to America that he determined to find and remove his mother's remains from an abandoned cemetery.

The following is an excerpt from a letter (December 2, 1892) written to his wife, Carmelite, in Turkey, in which he describes finding his mother's grave, who died in childbirth with her unborn child.

Precious Relics

The old cemetery is in a very bad condition
having been closed as a cemetery 30 years ago.
All grass grown, walks obliterated:
and now covered with six inches of snow.

None of us ever knew where our Mother's grave was.
Upon the cemetery plan was "Block 52, lot 2."
My heart leaped when I saw it.
But as no measurement were given in the rude plan,

Mr. Ford and I had to lay out the cemetery anew.
After two hours' futile work, we noticed a rounded
grave which we had thought just outside the lot.
A grave made forty two years ago could scarce have
retained its form, we thot. But finding absolutely

that no other grave had been made within the limits,
we made careful measurements, and found that the mound
was just inside as no other person had ever,

to my knowledge, been buried in the "Cristy" lot, there
was good ground for thinking this was our Mothers'
—So we set the men to work: 18 inches down, the
spades broke through into a hole. This had been caused

by the falling in of the top of the coffin. But the
arch of the top of the grave, well sodded as it was,
had stood all these years like a bridge—Mr. Ford went
away then to make with his own hands a nice box for the

precious relics. Soon we came on the rotted
fragments of the box, and of the coffin within.
Then I called the men out, and went down myself.
Carefully cleaning away the soil that had fallen

Precious Relics

into the coffin through the almost wholly destroyed
top, I worked down very near to where the bottom
of the coffin must be. But when at last my shovel
slipped along a Bone—my feelings overpowered me,

and I climbed out. Taking hold of the old German
sexton, I warned him earnestly, I enjoined upon him
the *utmost carefulness* and sent him down.
Beginning at the feet, he carefully lifted up

every precious relic on his shovel—
picking them out of the dirt and handing them up to me.
I put them in a large pasteboard box—two feet long—
borrowed from the College, as Mr. F. had not come back.

Then he would throw out the dirt to a spot
where I had the other two men stationed,
who carefully went through it with their fingers
and handed me every small fragment that had escaped

the sexton's eye. The bones were in excellant
condition, and we got *every one*—Most wonderful
and most touching of all, and giving convincing proof
that we were right,—in the pelvic region were

the skull and the wee bones of an infant.
Oh, how tenderly I laid them by themselves
in the end of the box: he that might now have been
a man, forty-two years of age.

Precious Relics

The skull no thicker than an eggshell.
But the little bones were strong and complete.
Then the skull of the Mother gave additional proof.
It was large—21 inches around the occiput,

the teeth were perfect in the lower jaw:
in the upper one, a tooth had been lost during life,
(one of the molars), one was partly decayed, and one
had fallen out after death—I found it amid the dirt—

with these exceptions the upper row was perfect.
The facial angle is the same as that of her sons.
At the top and back of the head was the "double crown"
that you have so often noted on mine; and in front,

near the forehead, on top of the head, a slight hollow or flatness just as in my head.—How can I describe my feelings as I held that dear head between my hands.— We had already selected a grave in a lovely spot in

Oakhill Cemetery. The sexton went away to prepare it. We carried the precious relics, now in a new box made by Mr. Ford, to the house of good Dr. Whyte until all should be ready: and at 2:30, Mr. Humphrey—the Sec'y

and Treasurer of the Oakhill Association, brought a double carriage. Mr. Ford and I got in with the box. Mr. H. drove us to the beautiful cemetery: and lowering the box into the grave, I sprinkled a few shovels full

of earth upon it, offered a silent prayer,—and asked the sexton to do the rest.

X. Anne Grant Barry, 1826–1906: The Woman Who Haunts Me: Great-Grandmother

Anne Grant Barry, 1826–1906

Years ago I heard from my mother the story of her grandmother, a strong woman who came to the raw country that became Minnesota. She was one of many women whose story became lost.

I have no photographs of her, only a few recollections from long-dead relatives, some entries on census pages, yet her story has continued to intrigue me. This I know: she left Ireland with a baby, and buried that baby from the ship carrying her and her husband, Edmund, to Quebec. When she was close to death in Quebec, her neighbors made her a brown scapular shroud to bury her, but she lived to die far from her homeland. When they came to Saint Paul, the shroud came with them. Of the many children she had, only eight lived to adulthood.

Each immigrant had a different story; not all hopes were fulfilled. For many, the rewards they hoped to obtain did not come until the second and third generation. By then the journey had faded. Succeeding generations lost the reasons why the ancestors came. Now we try hard to piece all the details together.

The Woman Who Haunts Me: Great-Grandmother Anne Grant Barry

A shadow figure, lost in anonymity and time,
like many of your sisters.
Scant traces of your life remain,
a few lines in old ledgers.

It is quiet now at St. Peter's
in this cemetery on the hill,
the Irish and French names,
faintly engraved on gravestones.
These are my roots, my ancestry,
a hundred and fifty years later.
You have no tombstone.
Not many remember you lived here.
Because you came, I am here;

one of your legacies.
Did you know you would never return,
see your brothers and sisters again?
Your family knew it was a one-way passage.
Was a wake held for you
before you left County Kilkenny?

Newly married, with courage
you climbed the gangplank,
baby Laurence in your arms
not knowing there would be one less
before you docked in Quebec.

The ship, with sails flapping,
creaked and swayed.
Friends and strangers crowded together;
lined the rails as a small bundle
was slipped over the side,

the first of the many children you would bury.
The damp cold penetrated your bones
and spirit that March 1846.

Chamberlain Street in Quebec, the Irish quarter.
Neighbors helped bury the unknown children,
made the brown scapular shroud for you.
You didn't die in childbirth,
an inner strength and faith sustained you.

Later, another long journey,
this time through rivers and lakes
with your husband, Edmund, and your son, Patrick
(and your shroud), brought you to Saint Paul.

Edmond wanted land for his children,
but the farm was an arduous life for you.
You were not a farmer's daughter.

The wolves howled in the wilderness
where you made your home.
For almost fifty years, seasons governed your life.
Hot, dry summers while the oats ripened
and dust seeped into the house.
The sounds of the animals,
the hum of the insects your only music.
And always, the green sky to watch,
when the clouds boiled out of their bounds.

Fall, its harvest of crops preserved
for the long snowbound winter.
The wind came then with different voices,
one creeping around the log cabin
finding chinks to be heard,
another cutting, a moan
to herald the coming blizzard,
all the while, inside, the clock's ticking

The Woman Who Haunts Me

and children's voices the only sounds
to break the short winter day.
How desperately you waited for spring,
remembering the softness of your girlhood,
waiting for the balmy wind to mellow your life,
far from Ireland.

For twenty-five years you had children who did not stay,
Ann, Margaret, Mary, Denis, the two Williams,
you survived the deaths of twelve of them.
Journeyed to this cemetery many times
to fill small graves not recorded.
Eight sons lived, one, my grandfather, Edward.

You and your great granddaughter,
both small women, living in diverse times
faced challenges in our lives.
Could I have survived your life

with its hard physical work,
isolation and loneliness,
and childbearing so often?
How painful to have children die,
never having known them.

You were eighty when you made your final journey.
I will, in the end,
share this common ground,
this field that holds families together
with a bond time cannot dispute.

XI. Carmelite Brewer Christie, 1852–1931: A Pandemonium of Sound

Carmelite Brewer Christie, 1852–1931

Carmelite Brewer was educated and well-prepared for her role as a missionary's wife. This woman of strong principles and strength under the most trying conditions was born April 25, 1852, in Lee Center, Illinois, the daughter of a minister and farmer, James, and his wife, Eliza (Pratt) Brewer. She attended Rockford Seminary (Illinois) graduating in June 1871. She taught school in Lee Center until her marriage to Thomas Christie on March 14, 1872.

Her life as a wife of a missionary called upon all her remarkable qualities as a manager and teacher. She often was in charge of the mission and school when Thomas visited outlying missionary stations and when he was gone on his many fund-raising trips to England and America. The doors to many wealthy homes were opened to missionaries, and they were accepted into society as people of noble calling.

During all this time, she managed a home for her five children. Missionaries sent their children back to England or America for their later education. She returned to the United States twice to establish a home in Beloit, Wisconsin, while they were in school. A missionary's life was not without its toll on family life. Her daughter

Carmelite Christie

From the Thomas and
Carmelite Christie and Family
Papers

*reproduced with permission of
Minnesota Historical Society*

Jean could not remember when the whole family lived under one roof. When her daughter Anna died in 1910 it had been fourteen years since she had seen her mother.

Although St. Paul Institute educated young men, she saw opportunities for the instruction and education of women. She worked with the local women to help ease the conditions in which they lived, socially, economically, and politically. In a culture that did not recognize the rights of women, she occupied a place of respect and authority.

Perhaps her greatest challenges were the Armenian massacres of 1895, 1909, and 1915. The history of the Armenians and Turks was a long and bitter one. In the 1909 event, she lost a son-in-law; the husband of her daughter, Mary, was killed as he tried to help a refugee. During 1915, she was left alone in St. Paul's Institute to run the school when Thomas was not allowed back into Tarsus by the authorities.

Her diaries relate the terrible misery during these times. Even to set down the words put her at risk. She kept the diaries under the floorboards, hidden from the authorities. She was, at this time, the only American in Tarsus. The following are direct quotes taken from her diary written during the Armenian Massacre of 1915.

From the Thomas and Carmelite Christie and Family Papers

reproduced with permission of Minnesota Historical Society

A Pandemonium of Sound

Tarsus, Turkey
August 15, 1915.

Such a day! I've given all day long and yet
   'twas but a drop in the ocean of misery.
      Such heart breaking cases! Our cook Partan's

sister came with a tale of woe and utter discouragement.
   I gave her a few praster and promised more help
      tomorrow. Her case was nothing compared with that

of mothers with young children. Several had left children
   too young or footsore to travel longer. These were left
      by the roadside to die! The mother was walking

Carmelite Christie
seated at desk,
Tarsus, Turkey

From the Thomas and
Carmelite Christie and Family
Papers

*reproduced with permission of
Minnesota Historical Society*

with five little ones to lead or carry.
> She gave up two! One woman with *four* (her husband in
> > military service) was sorely tempted to drop one.

She was on foot, all of them in rags. The baby had bowel
> trouble and not so much as a scrap of blanket
> > for any of them to sleep on. Of course I helped her

with road money, blankets and gave her children a lift
> just when she was feeling that she *could not* hold out
> > any longer. Two hundred and fifty Nigeh families

are in route. Many are penniless and hungry and footsore.
> *Pipi* a grad. of C.T.G.C. [Constantinople Girls College]
> > and her husband are among the refugees sent back

from Sulrarnel to go where they please and at their own
> expense. Pipi supported herself and husband doing
> > washing and ironing! They were well-to-do before.

Her uncle in Boston is very wealthy and would gladly
help if he knew of her distress, her brother too
is in America and doing well. Her cousin is in

the crowd and his two little children and another soon
to come. She walked all the way from Bozanta.
Her husband is in military service. She hasn't so

much as a bed or quilt for herself and children.
She can't carry things even if we give them.
So I might multiply tales of woe....

The day of reckoning is sure to come but our hearts
cry out "how long, oh Lord, how long."

A Pandemonium of Sound

August 19, 1915.

Another heart-trying day. Went to our church to see
   a few people in refuge there. One young married woman's
      dress was in such tatters, she could scarcely keep

it on (sent her a new gingham skirt). Some children sick
   and all the crowd half starved and filthy from long
      travel. Sent soap and fuel for them to wash

and bathe tomorrow. Later a white haired woman came to me.
   Had sold bedding and everything to pay. Kiva was hungry
      and penniless (give a medji and some food). Later

a blind man came led by his wife…have been driven out
   like cattle, goods seized and a few things sold
      for a small fraction of their value and more sold

or stolen along the way. (I helped a little) They were
very sweet and brave and asked nothing but were so
grateful for some ice tea. I gave a little money

and the tears ran down their faces as they left the yard.
Poor wronged sufferers. Surely God will help soon.
Three quite large children died from general

privation and exhaustion in the Armn [Armenian] church yard
this morning. There are deaths among these exiles
daily. Although they are being hurried on east

as fast as possible. A lot of the ill were taken to
the Turkish hospital. I suppose their friends can care
for them better there. Those in charge of the

hospital will not care to keep them alive. One child
in the church yard has smallpox! I am told that many
too ill to travel were left in Sultarniek to the

mercy of their enemies. Those who left were *forced* to
 hasten away. Who can bear to think of the anguish of
 heart of those forsaken loved ones and of the

feelings of those left under such circumstances.
 Our graduate Sadrak Akainian was taken from his church
 and school (which he was serving) and put into

the army. Officers came to him and asked, What are you
 doing here? "Teaching and preaching." We do not want
 teachers and preachers here, go into the army.

August 21, 1915

Have been over to our courtyard. Some very poor people
 are there & some rich ones. A lot of rich Nigeh people
 are in the boys school room. With crowds of men

sitting about visiting on the benches, a rather young
   & good looking woman lay in a bed on the floor nursing
      a one day old baby since her arrival. She was one

of the fortunate ones. Many women gave birth to children
   while on the train to Bozanta or in the carriages
      or on the roadside. Some babies died.

I found many women and children with sore eyes.
   One find was a nice old lady, clean & neatly dressed
      in black, her gelen and husband & five children

were with her. The old lady was a pastor's widow and tells
   of her three sons well-to-do in America. She had money
      & I helped her to find a house to rent for a short

time so she could be alone with her own people.
   She was most grateful. More deaths yesterday and today
      in the big church yard. The Armn. Priest of Zeitoon

A Pandemonium of Sound

    passed my window this morning en route for the station.
       His goods were on a donkey cart while he and his wife
         & children followed behind.

To be kind to a Teitoonli is almost a crime
    but I sent a boy after him with half napoleon.
       The family was so forlorn & I know are begging

their way along. Another group was of father & mother
    and two children, some years old. Each parent
       was carrying a child & one child was covered

with small pox scabs. The father called to our boys
    for help. I called to the boys to quickly give an oke
       of grapes on my account…I got two snaps of passing

exiles but as my films are old & the light not strong
    at six a.m. I dare not hope for much. To photograph
       such scenes is forbidden. I didn't go into the

From the Thomas and
Carmelite Christie and Family
Papers

*reproduced with permission of
Minnesota Historical Society*

A Pandemonium of Sound

Gregorian churchyard but could see through the door
    a *mass* of dirty wretched people & the crying
        of the babies, groans of the sick, shrill voices

of angry women & heavy voices of men in despair
    made a pandemoniun of sound.

View of Cloquet
after the fire.
October 12, 1918

*reproduced with permission of
Minnesota Historical Society*

XII. Recollections of Survivors of the Cloquet Fire: Flames Roared in the Wind: October 12, 1918

The Cloquet Fire

Firestorms can be created by men or nature; natural burnoff has always existed. When the weather is dry and humidity is low, conditions are set for disaster. These conditions control the intensity of the burn. It is almost impossible for us now to imagine the scope of this disaster, the total lack of resources. We do not remember a time without the equipment and professional manpower to fight fires. The smaller fires are contained. And when they cannot be, advanced warning systems are in place.

In October 1918 there were several fires burning separately for many days. Sparks from trains and dry conditions from that rainless fall combined to create conditions that grew to the dimensions of a firestorm. People in rural areas found escape blocked by roads gone to fire. Trains, not always able to get through, rescued many. Others were left behind to find refuge wherever they could. How appalling to see the flames and not be able to outrun them; to worry about the well-being of family and friends; to be totally helpless. Hundreds died.

But in that October, there was no help available. Heroes would appear in many forms with many faces.

Flames Roared in the Wind: October 12, 1918

Drought sucked moisture
all summer, turning woods and land
into papier mâché primed
for the torch of October.

Shot through with flaming red spikes.
The air, blue with smoke,
was hot and heavy, difficult to breath.

The Brookston train arrived
 Its weary refugees refused
to stay in Cloquet.
 "Too close to the fire."

When flames roared in the wind,
others knew their terror.
Panicked crowds filled the town,
fleeing all they knew.

Brightly illuminated stores ready
for Saturday night shoppers
stood rear guard
as the last people left Cloquet.
A ghost town ready to be consumed.

The lumberyard gave up its future:
houses, stores, and sheds.
Smoke billowed in dense clouds,
swirling to mask the road.

Trees exploded, their bark popped like corn,
showered the road with flaming kernels.
Fenceposts lighting the path to Hades.

Train whistles shrieked,
summoning all who could crowd
the flatcars and coaches.
Women and children first;
the tragedy of parting families.
Husbands were gentle with their wives,
with a tenderness
of a long forgotten love.
Leaving others trapped
in that death blaze.
Creeping along until on a high trestle
in Jay Cooke Park, it stopped.

Fire, licking from deep gullies,
turned rails to blistering threads
unsafe for its terrified cargo.
The only sound the hissing of water
cooling the rails.

Cautiously, the engine crawled
until asylum was reached.

A tall flaxen haired girl,
dressed only in flour sacks,
clutched two white-kid high-button shoes
filled with love letters
from France, the only articles
she was able to save.

A touring car fled the flames,
filled with frantic riders,
until the road ended too soon.
Children tumbled out,
against a wall of light,
clinging to each other.

Flames Roared in the Wind

Night came, in name only.,
The fury continued, advancing toward them.
Exhausted and sooty, they trudged,
found an escape from their nightmare.

She came, Mamie, a goddess of the night,
hair streaming out behind her,
her chariot a long potato wagon,
took reins into strong hands,
spurring horses through fire and wind,
until at last she thundered to safety.

The parents Koivista fought the firestorm
advancing toward their root cellar,
its contents their whole life.
Morning revealed their seven children
stilled forever.

Red Cross and National Guard with forest fire victims, Carlton County, October 1918

Photo by McKenzie

reproduced with permission of Minnesota Historical Society

Flames Roared in the Wind

Others perished in lakes and streams.
Arm pointing to the lake, the leader,
implored his followers to hurry
and remained a blackened arrow
never released.

Through it all, the sounds:
of doomed humans, of trapped animals,
of trees cracking and raging with
wind made of fire.

And then it was Sunday,
light and air filtered
through a sky made of smoke,
like a miracle Sunday dawned,
and the mourning began.

XIII. From the Papers of Ruth Mura Tanbara: American Born

From the Papers of Ruth Mura Tanbara

The paranoia after the bombing of Pearl Harbor took the form of forcing Japanese citizens to leave their homes and businesses on the West Coast. Many sold their businesses and possessions at a great loss financially. This evacuation scattered families and friends. Many did not return to their former homes after the war, but remained where they had settled. The irony that German-Americans and Italian-Americans were not suspected of subversive actions and not made to leave the West Coast did not go unnoticed.

The injustice and indignities foisted upon these citizens are difficult now for us to imagine. Many were educated professional people, successful merchants, and hardworking farmers. To be isolated in the barren areas of the West only added to their miseries.

The Japanese were not redressed financially until fifty years later when many had already died. Then the compensation was small.

reproduced with permission of Minnesota Historical Society

American Born

The Decree:
    "All persons of Japanese ancestry
        both alien and non alien,
  will be evacuated from the above area
        by 12 o'clock noon, P.W.T.,
        Tuesday, August 11, 1942."

I am not who you think I am.
I am an American
born and raised here.
I have done nothing wrong.

I leave all I have earned,
my friends, my honor.
I must sell my real estate,

my business, household goods,
automobiles, and livestock.
My piano for $15 dollars.
The junk wagon filled
with what I could not take.

We were marched to the train,
soldiers holding drawn bayonets
glinting in the sun,
lead our ragged parade.
I, who pride myself on my appearance,
can take only a small amount
of clothing and goods.

The Journey:

I am one of the tired Japanese,
crowded on the train.
The elderly people so fatigued,
they just turned their heads
to look out on the platform.

Many Nisei are just sprawled
on the chair cars, terribly neglected
in their personal tidiness,
for we had taken a roundabout route
and were on the trains for days.
It is not air conditioned.
Stale air filled with dirt.

We passed through the hot region
with one hour stop in the desert,
more than many could endure,
and many are "train sick."
I really realized this was war,
in its cruel reality,
 and we, Americans all,
were the enemies.

The Camp:

The wind, the wind,
it howls and blows whipping sand
to grate on my skin,
adding to the pain in my heart.

American Born

These centers where no one
wants to live are our destination.
They are not ready for us.
Few buildings and those
patterned after army barracks
hastily built with green wood
furnished with a stove,
straw to make mattresses,
and army blankets.
Dust, the "Arizona fog"
seeps through the crevices.

Vast distances of nothing greet us,
miles of barbed wire,
guard posts
(where would we run?)

Friends in other camps
live in converted horse stalls,
not cleaned thoroughly,
the smell when the ground gets wet
overpowering.
They eat in shifts of 2000.
There is no privacy,
two families to a large room.

Now I must appeal to you
my friend and former neighbor
to send us what I most need.
My studio couch,
stored in your garage.
My little cot is very uncomfortable,
the draft coming from underneath
is quite penetrating.
My coffee maker, a small radio,
my clarinet.

American Born

11:30 Christmas Eve 1942

I have opened your package
cookies, boots (my feet will be dry)
candy (there are no sweets here)
slippers, and stockings,
and 3 cakes of soap.
Five calendars
(how else to keep track of the time?).

Now a new year begins.
We try to carry on our duties,
live as a community.
Perhaps, someday, we will know
why we were considered aliens.
We are American born.
Why German and Italian Americans
were not sent away from their homes.

I hear the wind blowing,
the sands move in their own way,
covering the traces
that we live here.
Will someone remember us
and why we came,
not of our making,
or will we only be
ghosts of the past
that all want to forget.

XIV. The British War Relief Society: Dear Ladies of America

The British War Relief Society

In 1939, when war was declared between England and Germany, many women organized to send clothes and goods to the British Isles. The local committee was begun in May 1940 with headquarters at 501 and 511 Grand Avenue in St. Paul.

Elizabeth Ames Jackson and her sister, Margaret Ames Wright, carried on the tradition begun by their mother, Mary Leslie Ames, during the First World War, when the family was active with the Fatherless Children of France.

The organization's activities included cutting, sewing, knitting, remodeling used clothing, and packing for shipment to England. Tags with the maker's name were attached to garments and many wrote to thank the women for their help.

The following replies and a report are from the Charles W. Ames Family Papers.

The Germans have passed overhead; British children sit beside the ruin of their home.

British War Relief Society, New York

reproduced with permission of Minnesota Historical Society

Dear Ladies of America

I.
Elizabeth Ann, my daughter, was given
one of the loveliest dressed baby dolls,
sent for war orphans at Xmas time.

For myself, the doll meant so much more,
telling me of the kindness, understanding,
and sympathy of American women.

Dear Ladies of America,
I thank you so much for your gift,
a source of great pleasure to Elizabeth Ann
and a symbol to me.

II.
A report:
Young mothers and children,
dazed and so tired by the ordeal
they had been through,
had only the clothes on their backs.

Since clothing is rationed
people cannot spare clothes
so your 4 sacks of clothing
went a long way to give them relief.

The children were shy,
now they are a friendly happy group.
We had one baby,
he had lost both his parents,
a lovely little lad.
Through coming to the Settlement,

he has been adopted
and will have a comfortable home.

Box 228 arrived December 1941 in Edinburgh.
All garments received in good condition.
Plaid flannel blouses, nightgowns,
caps, dresses, bathrobes,
scarfs, sweaters and mufflers.
Evacuees come from other places
whom we are able to supply.
All the goods used to good advantage.

III.
Dear Madam, All we girls were overjoyed
with the clothes and Christmas presents.
They are some of the loveliest
things we could ask for.
We have been evacuated from Birmingham

and have been here twelve months.
Everything possible has been done
to make us happy. We hear from our parents
once a week and we write regularly.

We are very pleased to have a night's rest
away from the shelters and the raids.
The Welsh girls are very kind to us.
All we evacuees would be pleased
to have a pen friend in America.
Yours sincerely Florrie Felton.

IV.
I am a young woman, thirty years old.
Mother of two sons nine and six years.
My husband has been a prisoner of war
in Germany for nearly three years.

Dear Ladies of America

Today my sons and I went to a party
given by the American people
for Mothers and Children of Prisoners of War.
We had a lovely tea.
Each child was given a Xmas stocking
filled with sweets. The small children
had beautifully made woolly toys.

My boys had a large bag, each filled
with all manner of things.
It was a touching sight to see
all those Dear children
dipping into their bags.
My boys have just been tucked into bed.
They have their presents
on the table at their bedside.
I do want to thank you
from the bottom of my heart.

Corner of room, September 1940.

reproduced with permission of Minnesota Historical Society

I am afraid I do not write very well.
I hope all is well with you.
I am sincerely yours, Mrs. Robert Foreman.

V.
February 12, 1943
Dear Sirs, I am writing to thank you
for the gift you gave to my son
at the Party for Children of Prisoner of war.
He is six and rather thin for his age.

His Daddy is a prisoner in Germany
captured in May 1940
and working in a coal mine.
I don't think there is anything
I can let you know about this small family.

I stayed here through all the blitzes,
even when the roof and windows were
sailing away with the blasts of the bombs.
Thanking you once more
for your kind thoughts,
I remain, A. Webb (Mrs.)

To order additional copies of this book,
please send full amount plus $4.00 for
postage and handling for the first book and
50¢ for each additional book.

Send orders to:

Galde Press, Inc.

PO Box 460

Lakeville, Minnesota 55044-0460

Credit card orders call 1–800–777–3454

Phone (612) 891–5991 • Fax (612) 891–6091

Visit our website at http://www.galdepress.com

Write for our free catalog.